MY BLUE BOAT

Chris L. Demarest

Purple House Press   Kentucky

Published by **Purple House Press**
PO Box 787, Cynthiana, KY 41031

Read about more Classic Books for Kids at
www.purplehousepress.com

Library of Congress Cataloging-in-Publication Data
Demarest, Chris L.
My blue boat / Chris L. Demarest.—
〚20th anniversary edition〛.
    pages cm
Originally published: San Diego: Harcourt Brace, 1995.
Summary: While playing with a blue boat in the batthub,
a young girl imagines she is on an ocean voyage.
    ISBN 978-1-930900-76-9 (hardcover : alk. paper)
〚1. Boats and boating—Fiction. 2. Imagination—Fiction.
            3. Baths—Fiction.〛 I. Title.
PZ7.D3914My 2014
〚E〛—dc23
                                        2014015831

The illustrations in this book were done in watercolor
and india ink on watercolor paper. The display and
text type were set in Kennerly.

Printed in South Korea by PACOM
1 2 3 4 5 6 7 8 9 10
First Edition

To Bill and Margaret

My blue boat

catches the wind.

I sail past the sleeping town,

through the channel,

and into the busy harbor.

"Good morning," I call
to the fishing fleet.

My blue boat sails up

and down the swells

and across the wide ocean.

I dance with whales,

play tag with dolphins,

and steer through storms.

My blue boat dips under the moon

as I look for stars

and drift back toward the beacon...

and home.